For Edward & Scarlett
—G. S.

For Timothy, with love
—A. C.

First published in Great Britain in 2009 by Bloomsbury Publishing Plc.
Published in the United States in 2009 by Bloomsbury U.S.A. Children's Books
175 Fifth Avenue, New York, New York 10010

Library of Congress Cataloging-in-Publication Data
Shields, Gillian.
When the world is ready for bed / by Gillian Shields.—1st U.S. ed.
p.   cm.
Summary: Parent and child prepare for bed by cleaning up toys, folding clothes, talking about the events of the day, and reading a book.
ISBN-13: 978-1-59990-339-2 • ISBN-10: 1-59990-339-3 (hardcover)
ISBN-13: 978-1-59990-385-9 • ISBN-10: 1-59990-385-7 (reinforced)
[1. Stories in rhyme. 2. Bedtime—Fiction. 3. Parent and child—Fiction.] I. Title.
PZ8.3.S5538Wh 2009   [E]—dc22   2009002858

Typeset in Truesdell
Art created with watercolor

First U.S. Edition 2009
Printed in China by WKT Co. Ltd.
1 3 5 7 9 10 8 6 4 2 (hardcover)
1 3 5 7 9 10 8 6 4 2 (reinforced)

All papers used by Bloomsbury U.S.A. are natural, recyclable products
made from wood grown in well-managed forests. The manufacturing processes
conform to the environmental regulations of the country of origin.

When the World Is Ready for Bed

Gillian Shields

illustrated by Anna Currey

BLOOMSBURY

NEW YORK BERLIN LONDON

When the world
Is ready for bed,
The sky grows dark,
The sun glows red.

The little flowers
Shut their eyes,
The night birds sing
Their lullabies.

Supper's ready
In the pot—
Come and eat it
While it's hot.

Now clear the room
And tidy up;
There's a toy,
And here's a cup.

Let's talk about
The things you've done—
All the laughter,
All the fun.

Brush your teeth
And comb your hair.
Fold your clothes
Upon the chair.

Close the curtains,
Sleepyhead.
Find your blanket,
Cuddle Ted.

Pictures, stories,
One last look
At the tales
In one last book.

The lamp glows softly
On the stairs;
It's time for kisses,
Hugs, and prayers . . .

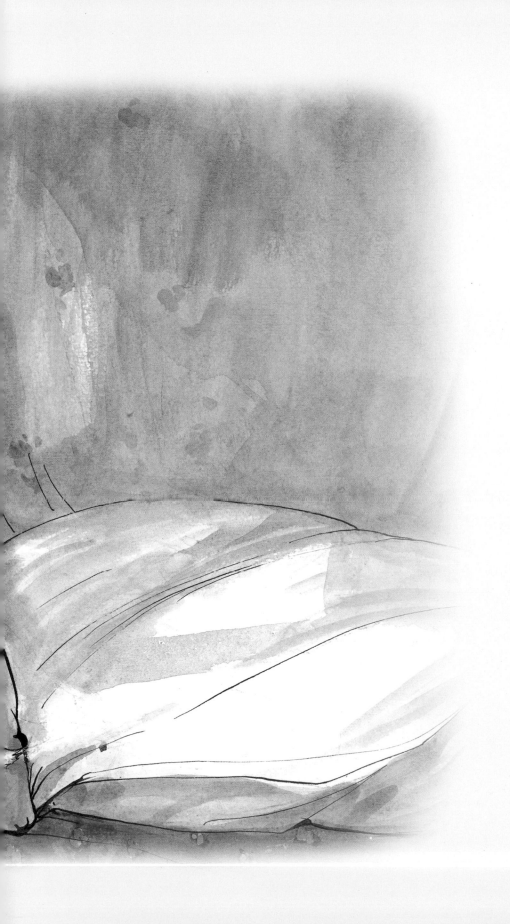

. . . And look! A star
Is shining bright,
To guard you
In the dreaming night.

Today has nearly
Slipped away;
Tomorrow brings
Another day.

Always lovely,
Always new,
Tomorrow's waiting
Just for you.